A
Web
of
Stories

Also by Grace Hallworth

Cric Crac
Listen to this Story
Mouth Open, Story Jump Out

Grace Hallworth

A
Web
of
Stories

MAMMOTH

TO SPIDERS EVERYWHERE

First published in Great Britain 1990
by Methuen Children's Books Ltd
Published 1994 by Mammoth
an imprint of Reed International Books Limited
Michelin House, 81 Fulham Road, London SW3 6RB

Reprinted 1995 (twice), 1996, 1997

Text copyright © 1990 Grace Hallworth
Illustrations copyright © 1990 Avril Turner

ISBN 0 7497 0553 1

A CIP catalogue record for this title
is available from the British Library

Printed and bound in Great Britain
by Cox & Wyman Ltd, Reading, Berkshire

CONTENTS

How the Web was Spun   7

1. How Spiders Became   13

2. The Strange Fate of Morning Glory   21

3. How Fire Came to Earth   43

4. Images in Bethlehem   59

5. The Wireenun in the Forest   75

6. Why Kwaku Ananse has a Narrow Waist   89

7. A Woven Testament   95

How the Web was Spun

Ever since I can remember I have been afraid of spiders, and as they thrive in abundance in the Caribbean where I grew up, I developed a special awareness of their peculiarities. But hand in hand with unreasonable fear is a grudging respect for these ungainly creatures which can be traced back to my eighth year, when I tried to prod a large spider from its perch on the ceiling towards a window, which opened on to a garden. The spider suddenly stopped running and turned on me – no doubt in exasperation for interrupting a Saturday afternoon siesta – putting *me* to flight.

I have watched spiders engage in life and death struggles against a swift-flowing tide of water in a drain, and a heaving wash of water in a bath-tub, and emerge triumphant. I have also seen spiders adopt ingenious forms of camouflage when they sense danger. Recently, I was filled with admiration for a tiny spider which accompanied us on a car journey from

England to Ireland (via ferry), and return journey after a fortnight's holiday of stormy nights and rainy days. Each day it could be seen repairing its web which was woven around one of the wing mirrors, in order to keep its larder stocked up.

When I came to England I had an idea that my environment would be spider-free. So I was horrified to find a large spider in the bath one morning. An examination of the underside of the tub revealed a den of spiders which swarmed forth as night fell for *el paseo*, a promenade across my living-room floor where they greeted each other with undisguised delight and cries of, 'Hi, Pete!' *Buenas noches, Dolores!* 'Whatcha doin,' Sid?'

On a cold Sunday afternoon as I lay reading my newspaper one of these characters dared to invade my bed. Under cover of the black fringes of a Welsh blanket it was stealthily working its way towards my pillow. The merest hint of movement caught my eye and alerted me to the approaching intruder.

Why do some spiders choose to live cheek by jowl with human beings while others prefer wide open spaces, or even an underwater environment?

Perhaps the answer lies in the way or ways human beings view spiders. Of all the creatures portrayed in literature, that of the spider is one of the most enigmatic and inspires a wealth of folk wisdom, cultural and religious beliefs which can be summed up in the rhyme:

> *'If you wish to live and thrive*
> *Let a spider run alive'.*

Surprisingly this attitude is shared by groups who hold widely differing world views and includes peoples of Europe, the Americas, the African continent, the land of Egypt, and the subcontinent of India.

In the story *Charlotte's Web* by E. B. White, the intrinsic qualities of spider are cleverly layered with those of daring and self-sacrifice typical of the heroic tale. When I shared this story with a class of first-year primary children I found myself so involved that for the first time I experienced love for a spider. The children confidently assured me that I would never fear spiders after meeting Charlotte. And I believed with all the faith of a new convert. A faith which was to be tested as soon as I came face to face with a large spider, when the fear reasserted itself, though not as strongly as before.

In exploring the universal mythology on spiders and linking it with my own observations I began to see how and why spiders have given rise to such a multiplicity of tales about their origins and interventions and I have tried to keep faith with both Charlotte and Arachne in *A Web of Stories*.

How Spiders Became

When Africans were taken to the
Caribbean, Kwaku Ananse became
Brer (Brother) Anansi, and although
many of the stories have their origins
in Africa they have been adapted to
reflect the new surroundings.
In this West Indian retelling Anansi
the trickster is out-smarted by
Tacooma and gets his come-uppance.

1
How Spiders Became

Brother Anansi was once a fine young man with a body as sleek and fat as a well-fed cat. At that time he owned a small parcel of land on which he grew mangoes, corn and coconuts. The field next to Anansi's belonged to the village chief who kept a herd of cows that he valued highly.

One morning Anansi found his land trampled up and his corn shoots destroyed.

'Wife,' he said, 'fetch me some smooth stones from the river. I intend to set mi mark on whoever trespassin' on my land.'

Late that night Anansi heard a scratching and a scrunching. He chose the largest stone and took a straight aim, and BIDIFF! something fell to the ground like a ripe mango.

Anansi ran to the spot. When he saw what it was he cried out, 'Oh mi lord, is one of the

13

chief's cow and it dead dead dead!'

He dragged the animal and hid it behind some bushes. Then he went into his ajoupa to tell his wife.

'Nansi,' she said, 'if the chief know you kill one of his cows, is death starin' you in yo' face.'

So the two of them talk till foreday morning and they come up with a plan.

That morning Anansi went to see his good friend. He said to him, 'Tacooma, I have a tree laden with ripe mangoes and I need help with picking the fruit before the birds spoil them. I will give you half of what we pick. Is it a deal?'

Tacooma agreed and Anansi took him to the tree and gave him a long stick.

'You start picking whilst I get two baskets for the mangoes,' said Anansi.

Tacooma start to shake the branches with the stick and BIDIFF! he see something big and brown fall out of the tree.

When Tacooma got close he saw that it was a large brown cow.

'Oh mi lord! what trouble is this for me. Is one of the chief's cows an' it stone dead!'

Anansi returned and saw the cow on the ground.

'Tacooma, what is this? Why yo' kill the chief's cow?' he asked.

Tacooma said, 'Anansi, I was picking the mangoes and the cow fall, BIDIFF! from the tree. Oh lord, what to do? What to do?' He began to wail and beat his head with his hands.

Anansi considered the matter. Then he said, 'Listen, Tacooma, is no use bawling and wailing. The chief always saying how he respects an honest man, and how he will forgive an honest man anything. So you take in front before in front take yo'. Go and confess to the chief that you kill the cow by accident before he find out. He bound to keep his word.'

And so with many assurances Anansi encouraged Tacooma to face up to the chief, and finally Tacooma agreed. But he said to Anansi, 'I must go home first and tell my wife what happen.'

'Well,' says Anansi, 'you better take the dead cow with you, else I might get blame for it.'

And Tacooma threw the cow over his shoulder and went home to his wife.

When he told her what had happened she said, 'Tacooma, how you so stupid man! You ever hear of cow climbing tree, dead or alive? You know how Anansi full of mischief and like to put people in trouble. Best we put our heads together and see what we should do.' They decided to do nothing.

Anansi wait, he wait, he wait. There was no

sign of Tacooma.

Finally Anansi decided to pay Tacooma a visit.

'Compere, what happen? What the chief say about the cow?' enquired Anansi.

Tacooma said, 'Is just as you say, Anansi. I tell the chief how the cow fall out of the tree an it dead. And he say, "Tacooma, you are an honest fellow and for that you deserve a reward. Keep the cow and make of it a feast." And that is just what I intend to do.'

Anansi said nothing but when he left Tacooma's house he went straight to the chief's compound and asked to see him. 'Chief, I have come about the cow Tacooma say he kill,' he announced.

The chief was puzzled but he knew how crafty Anansi was and decided to play dead to catch corbeau. The less he said the more he would learn about the matter.

'Tell me what *you* know about Tacooma and the cow and we will see whether it matches what *I* know,' said the chief.

So Anansi told how it was he who killed the cow and placed it in the mango tree.

When the chief heard what he had done he gave Anansi such a kick that he broke into a thousand small pieces which became spiders that ran to hide in dark corners, cracks and crevices. And there you will find them to this day.

So de wire bend
An my story end.

The Strange Fate of Morning Glory

In ancient times, the priests of Anahuác, the ancient land of Mexico, were also astronomers and studied the stars and planets as they moved across the sky. But on the eve of a new cycle of years, all the people of Anahuác watched the sky from sunset to sunrise. They feared that the god Morning Star who brought light to earth, might be held prisoner by his twin brother Evening Star, the god of

darkness, as he journeyed through the underworld.

I am grateful for the advice of Dr Elizabeth Baquedano, an archaeologist who specialises in the pre-Columbian archaeology of Mexico and teaches at the University of London, Department of Extra-mural Studies.

2
The Strange Fate of Morning Glory

Long long ago on the eve of the new year, there was a fierce battle between Morning Star and Evening Star. Each god wanted to overthrow the other so that he might rule the earth. Through the long night they fought until Morning Star was overpowered. Then Evening Star and his night demons bound the prisoner in a shroud, stifling daylight. As soon as the priests realised what was happening, they blew on their conch shells and beat drums to scare away the demons and free Morning Star. Novice priests climbed to the highest point of the Sacred Hill and kept the sacrificial flame burning. Everyone prayed to the great god Fire to aid Morning Star and rekindle the light.

Meanwhile, in the house of Chief Itzcoatzin, a midwife struggled in the black night to bring forth a baby. Hour after hour the chief's wife laboured in vain. The child would not come. The midwife dared not offend the gods by lighting the hearth fire until Morning Star was free. Instead she called to the slaves, 'Bring many rushes and surround the house with light. New life will not come into a world so cold and dark.' And the slaves did as she commanded.

Chief Itzcoatzin, a mighty and courageous ruler, hurried to the god-house.

'Offer a special prayer to the gods that they grant a safe birth for my child and health for my wife,' he said to the first priest he met.

'Tonight when all life trembles on the brink of destruction you would have us cease our prayers to the Great Spirit to save all mankind, for the sake of *two* lives!' rebuked the priest.

But the high priest overheard Itzcoatzin's plea.

He knew how long the chief had made sacrifices so that his wife might bear a child. He said to Itzcoatzin, 'Do not despair but go now to the temple of the priestesses and ask them to perform the dance for new birth.'

The chief went at once to the temple but the priestesses were at their lodge performing the dance for deliverance from darkness. So with a heart full of foreboding he returned home and offered his own prayers before a

cold empty hearth,
> 'O hai ya hai ya hai!
> Great god of wisdom
> God of life take pity
> O hai ya hai ya hai!
> Give life to my child
> Give life to my wife.
> O hai ya hai ya hai!
> Mother Earth who nurtures life
>   take pity
> O hai ya hai ya hai!
> Give life to my child
> Give life to my wife.'

As Itzcoatzin finished praying he heard a wailing sound. Even as it faded he heard the lusty cry of a baby. He ran to the room where his wife lay and found the midwife holding a squalling baby girl. But his joy was pierced with grief for his wife had sacrificed her life that the child might live. At that moment Morning Star burst through the night-shroud that bound him and all earth was made bright and beautiful with his golden radiance.

Now on that very day a sage, who had the gift of seeing, went to the high priest and said, 'As Morning Star broke from his prison I gazed upwards, and in the shape of the clouds, I saw a creature of which there is no likeness on earth.

23

It seemed to hang from the sky by a fine thread, right above the chief's house. And as it hung there I heard the cry of a new-born baby.'

The priest drew a sharp breath and said to the sage, 'Speak no more of this until I consult the Book of Fate to see what such a sign means for the child.'

Straightaway he went to the chief and asked, 'What name will you give the child?'

'I would name her Morning Glory for she was greeted by the glory of Morning Star,' replied the chief.

'Lest you offend the gods in your haste, wait and see whether they give a sign of her totem,' said the priest.

The priest hoped for a sign that would help him interpret the vision. It did not augur well for any child born at a time of such bitter conflict between the gods. When that child was the chief's daughter her future concerned everyone.

Many days passed and there was no sign, so the chief decided to hold the naming ceremony on the first favourable day, and although the priest was uneasy he could not forbid it.

In spite of the priest's doubts, the gods seemed to smile on Morning Glory. She learned quickly and excelled in all that she did. But her skill at spinning and weaving set her apart from the rest of the tribe for no one could weave such beautiful designs or spin such fine material. People came from every part of the country to see her work. Her father was proud of her skill but his greatest desire was to see her married to a man worthy of his noble family. Before he could get his wish he was struck down by a terrible plague which swept through the land.

When he was about to die the chief sent for the council of elders and said, 'I am troubled by many dreams and omens concerning my daughter. Give me your pledge that you will look after her, for she is young to be without counsel.'

'Do not fear,' said the elders, 'we will advise and direct her future.'

Then the chief called his daughter and said, 'Morning Glory, remember always that you come from a noble family. Live with honour and when death comes face it with courage.'

And Morning Glory swore this oath in the presence of the elders:

'Let the power of life and limb wither in me
if I dishonour the name of my ancestors.'

The plague had laid waste the land and weakened what it had not destroyed so Morning Glory went among the people comforting those who, like herself, had lost loved ones. She found homes for the homeless and distributed grain from her father's granary to the hungry. Her kindness found favour with the people.

As time went by and Morning Glory showed no sign of seeking a husband the counsellors grew anxious and it fell to the most senior of them to speak to her.

'Morning Glory,' he said, 'we are pleased that you follow in the footsteps of your father, the great cacique. The people are full of praise for your good works. Now it is time to choose a husband as your father wished.'

'My father also wanted a man who would honour the name of our family. I will choose only he who is worthy of my father's headpiece,' she replied.

'Must the people wait for a chief while you pick and choose? There is great danger for this land and for the people as long as there is no leader to fight our enemies,' retorted the counsellor.

'Then find me the cacique, the great chief who will govern wisely. Find me the warrior who will stand against our enemies with courage. Find him and I will marry.'

When the counsellor, and most respected of elders reported to the council what had passed between him and Morning Glory, they were stunned for not by word or by deed had she ever given any hint of such determination in the choice of a husband.

'Yet what she says is true. The plague has robbed us of the flower of our manhood and left us with a bunch of soft-bellied weaklings,' admitted one of the elders.

'Even if none of them is fit to be her husband and the father of our next chief she must still marry. The chief has to be of her line by birth or marriage,' said another.

'I sense that the girl's words are false,' stated the chief counsellor. 'Her manner tells me she does not wish to take a husband. There is more to her outburst than meets the eye.'

He sought the advice of the high priest.

'Since the girl will not choose for herself you must choose a husband for her, and soon. She has a duty to provide the people with a new chief so that the land may prosper and be secure,' said the priest.

The elders presented one suitor after another to Morning Glory. She would have none of them. Instead she made such a mockery of the men and their weaknesses in public that they fled from her presence. Some of them turned to drink from shame and leapt from the high mountains to their death. Very soon the queue of candidates ceased. There was no one who wished to marry Morning Glory. But her popularity with the people continued to grow. Daily she visited the market place to listen to complaints of those who had problems with the laws. Sometimes she gave advice, sometimes she argued with the court officials for people's rights and against the laws. The counsellors and court officials were dismayed at her boldness.

'Why do you defy the law and traditions of our land? Have they not served the tribe well?' they enquired.

Morning Glory answered their questions with her own.

'Why do the laws favour men above women? Do women not work in the fields beside men? Do they not give birth to the same warriors and priests whom you honour and respect?' she asked.

'Morning Glory, do not set yourself above the law. Your position will not save you from punishment if you do,' threatened the senior counsellor. 'You know well that in this tribe our laws follow custom and tradition, which even the great cacique respected.'

Morning Glory would not be put off by threats. Was she not the daughter of the greatest chief in all Anahuác? She would yield to no one.

She spoke in public that all might hear:

'The old men of the council would have us live the way of our grandparents while around us other tribes go forward and prosper. They wish to keep us in their power. Is it not time for a new council?' So skilfully did she argue the case against the counsellors, the people believed that her only thought was for their good. They called on the council to resign and a new council was formed.

However, it wasn't long before the people realised that the new counsellors were nothing but Morning Glory's lapdogs who barked as she ordered. Day after day the courts were filled with people complaining about injustices heaped on their heads. But there was no help for them anywhere. After a while none dared speak out, for fear of being cast into dark dank grottos far below the ground where many perished. At last they saw the true face of Morning Glory. Her ambition was clear for all to see. She wanted power. She was determined to be chief! She gathered around her a bodyguard who insisted that the slaves and all who belonged to the lowest castes must bend the knee before Morning Glory. She herself trained a large eagle-hawk to attack any who did not humble themselves before her. Wherever she went the eagle accompanied her, its keen eyes searching every corner.

In the market place there was much talk about the avenging bird. Gossip fed rumour and rumour kindled fear.

When the counsellors who had been dismissed saw how great was the suffering of the people, they visited the high priest secretly at night.

'We come not for ourselves, but for those who are yoked to the wheel of Morning Glory's folly. The new counsellors are her puppets and the council is a mockery,' said the chief counsellor.

30

yourself of *all* power and ask forgiveness of the elders you shamed publicly. Submit to their full authority, and live daily as the poorest peasant. Can you do this, child?' asked the priest.

Morning Glory's eyes were wide with disbelief.

'Do you ask *me*, a great chief's daughter, to become a peasant!' she exclaimed. 'You would see me shamed in front of the common people! No. Never! It would be more honourable to die!'

In vain the priest pleaded with her to return to the path of her ancestors but it was no use.

'You say I must make atonement and I will,' she vowed. 'I will cover myself with the needles of the cactus plant so that my blood flows. I will stand barefooted on the heated stones until the soles of my feet peel off like old skin from a snake. This and more I will offer but I cannot and will not crawl and beg.'

'Then you have sealed your own fate,' said the priest sadly. 'No one can help you now.'

After that it was as though demons of the dark places had taken possession of Morning Glory and were smothering every instinct of humanity, shutting off the light from her soul. She cared for nothing and for no one except her eagle which she encouraged in more vicious attacks. She would take the bird into the great square where the crowd was dense and gloat at the fear in people's eyes when they caught sight of the eagle. She would sneer at their clumsy movements as they hastened to bow and scrape. Yes, she would keep them full of fear for their fear gave her the power magic she needed to defeat the fearsome dream creature. The creature which sought to destroy her.

One day Morning Glory visited the square and saw a woman squatting on the ground. She was drawing pictures in the sand.

She called to the woman, 'Who are you that sits in the presence of the daughter of Chief Itzcoatzin?'

The woman stood up and faced the girl. She saw before her an old woman whose frail body looked as though it would crumble at the slightest touch. Her clothes were dirty and torn, and her hair unkempt. This woman was a stranger.

'Where do you come from?' enquired Morning Glory.

The woman made no reply but looked steadily at the girl.

'Do you not know that my eagle will tear you limb from limb if you do not humble yourself before me?'

The old woman turned her dark gaze on the eagle, and to everyone's surprise that fierce creature turned its head away and refused to attack. Suddenly it began to beat its wings wildly and, with a scream of anguish, launched itself in the air and flew away, soaring higher and higher until it was a speck in the sky. Morning Glory stood stunned and unbelieving. The eagle had been her constant companion for more than two years, and in that time she had trained it to obey her slightest gesture. For the first time it had disobeyed and shamed her. Angry beyond words she hurried to her house intending to kill the bird. When she got there it had disappeared.

She slept fitfully that night and her dreams were dominated by images full of foreboding. Pits of adders and rattlesnakes opened up before her, she came upon an abyss where there was only night. She dwelt in underground caves empty of people and heavy with silence. She was trapped in all these places. Again and again she cried out and her screams woke her from the nightmare.

Early the following morning Morning Glory rose and called her bodyguard.

'Come with me and arrest one who will not bend the knee.'

These men had seen what the eagle did to

those who provoked the anger of Morning Glory. They imagined that the culprit must be an idiot. When they arrived at the square a death-like silence greeted them. There was not a soul to be seen. Except the strange old woman. She was squatting in the same place as the day before.

'There is the one who would defy me,' cried Morning Glory. 'Take her and throw her into the deepest darkest pit where she can neither stand nor squat. Where there is nothing to feed on but insects. Where there is no water save the drops on the cold walls at night. There she will bend the knee until she dies.'

What did the men see before them? Just an old woman whose skin was caked with mud. The filthy rags barely covered her body. She was writing in the sand.

As they approached the woman stared at each man in turn. The men froze where they stood, their faces turned away from her eyes which pierced their hearts as if by a poisoned dart. Morning Glory had followed the men but did not know why they had suddenly stopped. She ranted at them, 'Cowards! Idiots! You call yourself braves yet cringe like hairless dogs before an old woman. I spit in your faces!'

They could not move to save their lives,

36

All night Morning Glory paced her room planning what she should do. There was no one else for her to command. None to aid her in her devilry. But she was poisoned with pride and evil and could not draw back.

'I will make the old woman show fear before the people before I kill her. I must conquer her or myself will die.' As she uttered these words, a shiver sharp and cold as a flint knife sliced through her body.

A crowd had gathered around the old woman who was once again drawing mysterious pictures in the sand. Some of the watchers said that she was describing a disaster still to happen, something which would change their lives. Others scoffed and said that the only disaster would be the death of the old woman if she refused to bend the knee to Morning Glory.

Suddenly Morning Glory was in their midst holding her father's war club. Its grooved sides were set with sharp flakes of obsidian. The people fell flat on their faces. All but one.

'So you are determined to defy me, old woman!' said Morning Glory. 'I am determined that you will bend the knee or die today.'

Slowly, very slowly the woman rose to her feet. As she moved her tattered clothes were transformed into snakes, scorpions and other crawling creatures of earth. In her long red hair were flowers of many colours. On her feet were enormous claws and her fingers were like talons. Deep-set in a nut-brown face were a pair of eyes which shone with a terrible brilliance that filled the city with a dazzling white light.

Morning Glory fell to the ground and waited for judgement.

'By your pride and folly you have caused great suffering among my people. They have cried out to me with their blood and tears, and I, goddess of Earth, have come to relieve their pain. In your lust for power you have broken a sacred oath to your father. You have spurned the help of old and wise. But you will not die!'

The voice sounded like a powerful wind rushing through the great forests of the high

mountains: 'Death is too honourable for what you have done. Instead you will live to know what it is like to be trodden underfoot, to be reviled, to be condemned to dark places. You will crawl on your belly, a creature of the dust. But you will keep the one virtue you possess, your spinning and weaving. And from your skill men and women will learn a craft which will be useful to all people and pleasing to the gods.'

When she had spoken, the goddess vanished.

And immediately darkness covered the land and the earth tumbled. For a brief moment the sky dipped and then rose into its rightful place. As the darkness cleared, the people saw a huge and hideous creature with long thin hairy legs and a round body. Its movements were hesitant and clumsy, and its small black eyes looked everywhere seeking escape.

The crowd scattered in fear. People threw stones to chase it, to kill it.

At last it found a small opening and forced itself into a hole in the ground to hide until night should fall.

Morning Glory had become a spider.

How Fire Came to Earth

*The getting of fire is a universal
theme in mythology. I have combined
elements from many other stories
about fire in this Cherokee myth.*

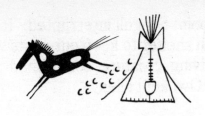

3
How Fire Came to Earth

At the beginning of time, long before man was formed, there was no fire on earth. Everywhere was cold and bleak and a grey mist shrouded land and sea. Woolly-coated creatures huddled together in caves and feathered ones clustered wherever they could find shelter. Some creatures made their homes in the ground while a few burrowed to the very depths of the earth and were never seen again.

High above earth the great Sunbird basked in the glow of a fire that burned day and night. He did not know of the suffering of earth creatures. His home was too far away. At last the creatures could bear the cold no longer so they held a meeting.

When all were gathered Leopard began: 'Two of my litter are dead from cold.'

At this point Seagull interrupted: 'It is hard to find enough shelter to keep our nests warm.'

Every living creature complained about the cold. Only Owl kept silent.

When all had spoken she said: 'Mighty Thunderbird shoots fire-sticks across the sky when he is angry. Let us ask him for some of his fire.'

They chose Eagle to seek him out for he could fly higher than any other creature. Besides Eagle knew where to find him. He flew to a mountain in the middle of the ocean where Thunderbird rested after his noisy outbursts. There he waited for many days. When Thunderbird arrived, Eagle approached him and said: 'Great one who makes thunder-fire, I come from earth where many creatures die from cold. Will you give some of your fire to warm earth?'

'My fire is for the sky,' replied Thunderbird. 'You could not use it on earth, but my brother has a fire tree. I will ask him to give you a branch from it.'

And he went at once to Sunbird and said: 'Brother, the wretched creatures on earth perish because of cold. Give them fire so that they may live!'

But Sunbird said: 'No, I will not give them fire. Their knowledge is not sufficient to guard it and they will destroy earth.'

Again and again Thunderbird pleaded for earth creatures but Sunbird would not yield.

One night when his brother was asleep, Thunderbird stole a branch from the fire tree. He fitted it to his bow and shot it down on to the mountain where he had met Eagle. It went straight to the heart of a dead sycamore tree and set it alight. Earth creatures saw the blazing mountain and were anxious to get hold of fire but Eagle was away and no one knew when he would return. One of them would have to cross the water to get to the blazing mountain before fire died away.

'Whooooo? W-hoohoo-hooo? Whoo will fly to get fire?' called Owl.

'I will. I will. I will fly to the mountain and bring back fire,' said a bird with beautiful silver-grey feathers. And off she flew across the sea. She had never flown so far or so high. She was buffeted by strong winds but held her course and flew steadily on.

On the mountain red-hot flames leapt and crackled and the bird could find no place to alight. She would have to seize a fire-stick and return at once. Round and round she flew looking for an opening but as she drew near fire, a change came over her. She felt a tingling, prickling sensation. Grey-black wisps curled and twisted around her eyes and snaked into her mouth. She tried to escape by flying high above them and the cool clean air cleared her eyes and helped her to breathe.

In her breast, the bird felt that she must soon leave, for the struggle with fire had tired her. Cautiously she dropped to a lower air stream just above fire, where the wisps were small and weak. Once more sharp pains shot through her body and as the stabbing pains increased, her

46

feathers began to fall off. 'Haaargh! Haaargh! Haaargh!' Her harsh cries of pain and fear came from a throat sore from heat and smoke. Her wings were badly burnt and the skin on her feet hung like strips of yellow ribbon. She mustered all her strength and lifted herself up and away. She was fortunate that the wind was blowing in the direction of the Homeland. She flew low and spray from the waves soothed her aching body.

At the water's edge the creatures were waiting for the bird to return with fire. Instead, they saw a bedraggled creature with eyes as red as fire itself. Her silvery feathers were blackened. And they have remained that way to this day for she had become the bird we now call the Raven.

'Huu did this to you?' howled Wolf.

'It was fire himself. He stabs with sharp points while his wisps force your eyes shut and squeeze breath from your body. We cannot tame fire,' said the bird.

'I can. No one is swifter than I. I will, I will, I will go to the mountain and seize fire,' boasted Leopard. Immediately he dived into the sea and started to swim across the wide expanse of cold water. Waves as tall as Leopard tossed him about. Swift treacherous currents tried to pull him under but his strokes were powerful.

On the mountain the fire blazed.

Leopard decided to swim around and see where he could best attack fire. He found a winding path that led to the top of the mountain. Suddenly he was enveloped in a thick black cloud which began to smother him. His eyes hurt so much that he couldn't see. Frantically he spun round and round trying to escape but fire was choking the breath from his body. He was beginning to weaken when he saw a golden light and rushed through the light which had a sting fiercer than bees robbed of their honey.

He roared a fearful roar, leapt into the air and fell headlong into the sea. It was the cold water that saved him, cooling his feet, his body, his face.

Leopard hurt badly all over. His fur was singed and his legs were stiff. Partly floating and partly swimming he made his way back home. The creatures were so sure that Leopard would bring fire that they had prepared a large pit in the forest which they filled with leaves and dried seaweed.

'We will tame fire and keep him alive here. Then every creature may take some of fire whenever there is need,' said Owl.

As they waited at the water's edge for Leopard, they talked of all the things they would do when they had fire.

But what was this?

Could this be graceful Leopard so fleet of foot!

The creatures could not believe their eyes. Leopard's beautiful golden coat was now threadbare and spotted with black soot. They watched in amazement as he limped away into the forest.

Night, the black curtain, fell and still fire blazed.

From a distance earth creatures watched, glad at least for the warmth that came from fire's brightness.

Who dared to fetch fire now that powerful Leopard had failed?

'WhoooooOOO? W-hoo-hoo-hooooo? Whoo ooooooo?' Owl's mournful cries echoed through the night.

'Let me! Let me! Let me fly to the mountain,' pleaded Bat.

She had been asleep for most of the day. Now she was wide awake.

No one heard Bat's gentle twittering. No one saw the small black creature fly off in the dark. She had no fear of the journey for she was used to travelling long distances and the thought of bringing back fire spurred her on. As she approached the mountain she saw fires flare up like rockets showering sparks everywhere. Bat was spellbound by the bright colours. She flew close yet felt no pain from fire's light. She darted down to seize a twig of fire and it spat a bunch of sparks right in her eyes. Shrieking she rose in the air flying blind for her eyes were badly burnt.

'Can't see! Can't see! Can't see!' she cried.

'Seeseeseek! Seeseeseek! Seeseeseek!'

keened the other bats who heard her cry of distress. Their high-pitched calls helped her to find the way back to the Homeland and the creatures who anxiously waited at the water's edge. All gathered around to see what fire had done to Bat.

'Fire paints bright pictures but when you try to take them he throws dust in your eyes. Fire is cruel,' sobbed Bat.

And ever since that night Bat has been blind. She shuns the light of day and lives in dark places.

Snake scolded. 'Iss s-s-so small a creature that s-s-sets out to s-s-steal fire! There muss be no more of thisss folissness. I will s-s-seek fire if Eagle isss not back s-s-soon.'

Now Spider was going to tell the other creatures about her idea to catch fire and bring him back. But when she heard Snake scolding Bat she said nothing. Instead she crawled away to work on her plan. She would build a bridge across the sea to the mountain and fetch fire. She began to weave a pattern which she had practised so often that she could do the movement in her sleep. As she spun she sang a song:

> 'In and out and in and out
> Up and down and round about

In and out and in and out
Pay the silken thread far out.'

Again and again she repeated the movements as she sang. Hour after hour she spun her strong silken thread and payed it out. At last her feet touched ground. She had arrived.

Spider scurried around looking for something to catch fire. It must be

something flat that would sit on her back
something that would not let water in
something that would not let fire out.

Near the water she found a flat stone but it could not hold fire in.

Further along the beach she saw a piece of wood. Fire had burnt a hole through it.

Dawn flooded the sky reflecting the colours of fire below.

Spider searched everywhere.

Half-buried in the sand she saw a shell. It was flat enough to sit on her back and hollow enough to keep fire in and water out. Spider carried it to where fire was burning brightest.

Phtt! Phtt! A small piece of burning wood broke off from a branch and flew into the shell. At once Spider placed the shell on her back and set out for the bridge she had woven. When she got there fire had destroyed the silken bridge.

She didn't know what to do. Fire was spreading and soon there would be no place to

stand. There was no other way out. She would have to go into the sea.

But Spider couldn't swim!

Then she remembered that whenever she saw the tide coming in at dawn, it flowed gently in to shore. Could she risk going into the sea with fire on her back? She would have to hurry for already she could see a faint glow of morning light through the night curtain. Quickly she spun a sticky bell-shaped web under her body to keep her afloat. She stepped bravely into the sea.

All morning Spider floated on the gentle

tide-stream towards Homeland. She was sleepy and tired but dared not sleep for she didn't know when the tide might become choppy and fast. She sang a song to keep her awake:

'Rock and sway and rock and sway
Tide-stream flow-in all the way
Rock and sway and rock and sway
Fire safe from briny spray.'

At last the tide washed her up on the shore where she had left the others. All the creatures had gone home! There was no one to greet Spider or to lift the shell off her back. She struggled up the beach and along the path to the pit in the forest. But now, fire was beginning to burn through the shell and Spider could feel the heat on her back and the hairs of her legs. At last she could bear the pain no more. She tilted fire on the ground and curled up in a tight ball to protect herself. Greedily, fire licked the ground around the frightened creature ready to devour her. And he would have done so but Eagle returned just then and saw what was happening. He swooped down and gripped Spider in his talons and took her away to safety near the forest pool.

And so it was that this tiny creature conquered fire and brought it to the Homeland so that all earth's creatures might have warmth. Spider knows that fire lurks in the forest waiting for a chance to punish her so she lives in water where fire cannot reach her. The water spider still carries the splash of colour where fire marked her.

Images in Bethlehem

This story was inspired by a legend I read many years ago. Since then I have found a rich vein of similar legends from many parts of the world. David is said to have escaped from Saul because of a spider's web, and Mohammed was saved from his enemies, as was Felix, a priest of Naples later to become a saint.

4
Images in Bethlehem

They came to Bethlehem at dusk
A man, a woman on an ass
Gently he lifted her from its back
She swayed unsteady on her feet
*   and clung to him*
For a moment they stood
Three figures etched against the canvas of a
*   darkening sky like silhouettes.*

I came out of the inn and saw the travellers near the well.

'Shalom!' the man greeted me. 'Good friend, will you stay with Mary my wife, while I speak with the inn-keeper?'

'Master,' I said, 'if you seek lodging you will not find any here. Even on the cold floor of the

59

cook-house travellers spread their sleeping mats at night.'

But the man would not be put off.

'I must try for my wife's sake,' he said. 'She is weak from the journey and needs rest.'

And he hurried into the inn.

Mary's eyes were gentle and wise beyond her years. I think that she was not much older than my thirteen years. The man could have been father to her. I sat down beside her on the resting stone.

'I am Naomi and work here at the inn. Have you journeyed far?'

'Five days we have been on the road from Nazareth. After the second day of our journey, Joseph's mule was stolen and he is weary and footsore, though he tries to hide it from me.'

'Have you no friends in Bethlehem where you might find shelter?' I asked.

'Oh yes,' she answered, 'we shall stay with Joseph's family in the city but we need a place to rest tonight.'

We saw Joseph coming and rose to meet him.

'Mary, my beloved, we must go on to the next inn. There is no room here,' he said.

'The next inn!' I exclaimed. I looked at the three travellers. The man's eyes were red-rimmed from lack of sleep, the woman was big with child, and the donkey! Well, they would be robbed, or worse, just for that bag of bones of a donkey. They wouldn't get as far as the next village and that was closer than the next inn. I made up my mind.

'Come with me,' I said. 'I have a shelter close by. There you'll be safe and warm for the night.'

My lantern's thin beam of light pointed the way through pine forest and up a rough narrow track. On either side there were steep rock walls honeycombed with caves. My cave was the last and well-hid. Even in the light of day you could pass the entrance and not see it. The cave was dark and cold when we entered. Maybe it would seem frightening to a stranger but since my mother had died and left me an orphan, it was home to me. I knew every step of ground and patch of wall in it. I kindled a fire and soon the cave was warm and bright. The animals – a cow and its calf, a ram and two ewes – had settled down for the night but when the donkey ambled across to join them they made room for it.

'Are these your animals?' asked Joseph.

'No,' I said, 'when I found the cave they were already here. We share in peace.'

We supped well on a loaf of bread and chunks of fish baked with olives I had brought with me from the inn. Afterwards we drank fresh goat's milk and ate some dates. I offered them my bed made with pine branches and hay. Every week I changed the hay so the bed was sweet and clean.

'Where will *you* sleep?' Mary asked.

'I will be warm enough near the animals. I often sleep with them when the nights are cold,' I said. And that was the truth.

She hugged and kissed me. Joseph put his hands on my head and said, 'Peace be with you always, Naomi. You have fed and sheltered, and even given your bed to strangers.'

He took some bedding from a bundle and laid a blanket over the branches and hay for Mary to lie on. He spread another over her to keep her warm. Then he laid himself down on his sleeping mat.

Soon there was only the sound of crackling as the fire-wood burned.

There was peace in the cave.

The hills of Bethlehem resound
with rhapsodies from distant spheres
a paean of peace and joy
And hosts of angels from on high
swirling and whirling like dervishes
in a dance of ecstasy
worship a baby boy.

Next morning I said to Joseph, 'Master, I can see that Mary will soon give birth. Rest here awhile for her sake.'

It was well that he agreed for on that very night the child was born. And what a night it was!

When the animals heard the baby crying they crowded around.

At once the child began to make happy sounds as though he was laughing and talking with the animals. Then they knelt down before the baby and made *their* noises. To hear them you would have thought they were trying to sing a lullaby.

In the midst of all this we heard a scuffling sound outside the cave and a man entered carrying a lamb. When he saw us he drew back and said, 'I didn't know that anyone lived here. My flock grazes on the meadows beyond the hills above. I heard the cries of animals and came to see whether any of mine had strayed.'

I welcomed him and showed him the animals kneeling around the baby.

'Glory be! What kind of child is this that animals kneel before him?' he asked in wonder.

'You come in time to celebrate our son's birth,' said Joseph. 'Will you share some mead with us?'

'Gladly,' said the shepherd, 'and offer as a gift my lamb who followed me of her own accord.'

Suddenly the animals ceased their cries.

There was a great stillness.

The fire I had lit earlier was dying but the cave was flooded with a light so bright that there was not a dark place or shadow in it. As I looked around I saw that each face shone as though it was lit up from inside, and the baby was bathed in a golden glow. All the lines of pain had gone from around Mary's eyes and they were soft with love.

The shepherd broke the silence.

'Strange! I came here weary and cold from tramping the hills. Now, I want to run and leap and shout for joy. What has happened? I have never felt like this.'

'The mead was strong and makes us merry and light of spirit,' I said. Yet even as I said it I knew that was not the reason. And Mary smiled as though she held a secret too precious to share with us.

'What will you call your son?'

'His name is Jeshua,' said Mary.

'A name that is rightly his,' said the shepherd, 'for I believe that he is the One who will bring salvation to his people, as it has been foretold by the prophets.'

And everyone present was filled with joy that night, and marvelled.

To Bethlehem the Magi came
following a bright new star.
It hung o'er hillside bleak and bare
*   an iridescent pearl*
*   guiding true seekers on the way*
*   to a lowly stall whereon the Christ child lay*
*   in perfect bliss.*

It was just seven days after the birth of Jeshua that three strangers came to the inn. I could see from their clothes and manner that they were important men, and wealthy too with all their following of servants.

They said that they were seeking a baby. This was no ordinary child but a great king and saviour. They offered a reward to anyone who knew of a baby born within the month. I was sure that they were looking for Mary's baby. I had not told anyone at the inn about the birth, so when the men left I followed them and told them all that had happened on the night that Jeshua was born. They got very excited and asked me to lead them to the cave.

When they entered the cave the men greeted Mary and Joseph as though they were great people and knelt before the baby, just as the animals did on the night of his birth.

'We have travelled through many lands to find this child who is destined for greatness,' said

66

one who appeared to be the eldest.

'Master, they say that the strange light we saw in the cave came from a special star that appears when a great king is born,' I said.

'My wife has been forewarned that the child will be a true rabbi of Jehovah,' said Joseph. 'But now you talk about a great king!'

'Josephus, we cannot tell you why or how these things will come to pass, for even the wisest of us is but a fool in the presence of the great power that rules the universe.'

They all believed in the movements of the planets and were able to predict events according to these movements. Each had seen the special star and knew what it meant so they had set out on a quest. They brought with them gifts for the baby. There were casks of polished wood which held sweet-smelling perfumes, myrrh and frankincense, and a casket in which there was a crown of gold set with diamonds and precious stones.

We were tongue-tied at the sight of such wonderful gifts. Then Mary spoke and there was something in her voice I had not heard before. A sort of pride.

'Wise and noble lords who have journeyed so far to pay homage to our son,' she said, 'we rejoice at the tidings you bring and are honoured by these gifts so costly and so rare. All that has happened here we will guard in our hearts and reveal to Jeshua when he is old enough to understand.'

Before they left the men drew Master and myself aside and said, 'King Herod asked us to let him know as soon as we found the child but we have been disturbed by dreams and omens. We believe that he intends harm to the child. You must leave this place as soon as you can. And you, Naomi, must tell no one where the child is.'

The Master believed the men because they seemed so wise, and he feared for his son's life but Mary never doubted that what had been prophesied would be fulfilled.

Early the following morning Master said, 'Naomi, today I shall go to the city to visit my family so that they may prepare a place of safety for us.'

I was uneasy about leaving Mary and the baby alone so I said, 'I will stay here while you are gone. When you leave cover the entrance with branches from the myrtle tree so that it is hidden.'

Master never got to the city.

He told us that on his way there he saw soldiers pursuing mothers who were trying to find hiding places for their babies. He said that when he saw the mangled bodies of babies lying in his path he turned around and started back to the cave.

Meanwhile, Mary and I did not know what was happening outside until we heard the tramp of boots and shouting of men's voices. I knew at once that they were soldiers searching the caves. There was no telling what they might find in some of them for it was rumoured that robbers and murderers used the caves as a hide-out.

I showed Mary a niche at the back of our cave where she could hide the child and we hid all signs of a baby's presence. Mary sat quietly whilst I went to the entrance to listen for sounds of footsteps coming our way.

There were just two of them.

'Let us look closely. There may be something behind the branches,' said one soldier.

'How could anyone get past such a web and not disturb it?' asked the other. 'Look at the layers of webbing, man! That must have taken many days to spin. What a beauty!'

This soldier seemed more interested in the spider's web than looking for a baby.

'But if there was more than one spider the web could have been made in a few hours,' persisted the first soldier.

'Nay, there is but one weaver. A lone spider

and there he is,' said the other. 'Besides there is a sign here that means danger. Let it be.'

I heard them walking away but did not breathe until their footsteps faded. Mary and I wondered though, what he meant by a sign of danger, but we dared not go out of the cave in case other soldiers were about.

It seemed a long time after that the Master returned. He came in quietly and was as pale as the waning moon.

He said he would never forget the faces of the dead children, the sound of mothers weeping and the fathers' curses as they watched the slaughter of their innocent children.

Nor would he forget what he saw outside the cave when he returned. He described the enormous web a spider had woven that morning. A web that covered the branches he had placed in front of the entrance and the area all around it. And most amazing of all, was the sign of a cross beneath the webbing! A sign which meant danger for the soldiers but salvation for Jeshua and his parents.

A tiny spider, one of the smallest of creatures, helped to save the life of the Christ child.

The inn is packed at this time of year. Now that it belongs to me I turn no one away who wishes to stay. And each year on the night of Jeshua's birth I tell the story to those who are here. And strange to say, each year on this night, a spider spins a web over the door of the cave.

The Wireenun in the Forest

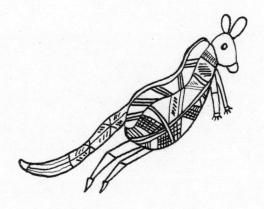

Many years ago while visiting Australia to take part in a storytelling festival I heard an outline of a legend about a woman who preyed on the men of her tribe. Later on I read a very short story in a collection of legends called Aboriginal Myths and Legends selected by Roland Robinson (pub. Hamlyn, 1968). Both versions lingered in my mind and grew into this retelling.

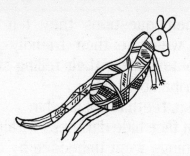

5
The Wireenun in the Forest

In the Dreamtime, the land of Australia was fresh and green. Mountains of dense tropical forests climbed down to meet fertile savannahs which rolled and dipped and yielded to lush swamps, and to the everchanging sea.

The first people were the Aborigines and many tribes roamed the land. Men hunted and fished, women dug for food in the ground. Children swam in the rivers and speared snakes in the billabongs. At night everyone gathered around the campfire to dance and share stories.

Now in a certain tribe there was a young woman who did not care about dancing or sharing stories. She lived apart from the tribe and made her home in the forest. At first the women of the tribe visited her but after a while they stopped. Although she smiled and answered their questions they felt that she didn't really welcome their friendly gestures. The wise women threw their telling stones and warned the tribe about her:

'All skin teeth is not laughin'
Bright face hide darkness within.'

Their warnings went unheeded by the young men for they thought they knew better than their elders.

After all, were they not hunters and warriors skilled in reading signs of danger?

'Even as sun and moon cannot share the same sky, so too with old and young,' sneered one warrior.

And a chorus of praise for the woman rose from the men's lips as sweetly as the morning song from birds of the forest.

'Her eyes are bright, bright as campfire that greets weary traveller,' said one man.

'Ah!' sighed an unmarried hunter. 'None can match her. She is beautiful to look upon.'

'Yet she has no friends among our women,' reflected Burryan, the great warrior.

At these words a few of the men nodded wisely but many wanted to believe that the young woman was as good as she was beautiful.

It happened that one day a blackfellow went to hunt for game. His search led him into the depths of the forest. By the time the hunter had

tracked and killed the animal it was late in the day. As he was walking through the forest he met the young woman. She greeted him:

'It is a good day, hunter. Your catch will provide a great feast tonight.'

'Will you not come with me to camp and share our fire?' asked the hunter.

'I cannot come tonight but let you and I make a small feast of thanks at my fire,' said the woman.

77

'Na! Night falls quickly and there are many steps to camp,' said the hunter.

But the woman persisted:

'See in fire-hole wild pig bakes
Yams and sweet potatoes wait in fire-stones
See in vessel, juice from palm bubbles
Truly a feast for brave hunter.'

The hunter was thinking. What a story he would have to tell that night around the campfire!

He agreed and followed her as meekly as a newborn lamb follows its mother.

She spread the baked-hot meal before him and kept his goblet filled with frothy juice. Each time he rose to leave she pressed him to stay:

'Let you rest near fire-stone
Soon you leave with quick quick steps
Soon you run so high, so light
Soon you go into the night.'

Poor hunter! The cloying drink and the warm fire weakened his body and addled his senses.

'Wake me,' he mumbled, 'as day breaks night.'

'Sa, Sa,' agreed the woman.

Almost at once the hunter fell into a sleep as deep as death itself. No sooner did his snores fill the room than the woman went a little way from her shelter and took hold of a gunai, her wooden digging-stick. She sharpened one end of it to a point. Back she crept to the place where the man lay and drove the pointed end straight into his heart. He died at once. Then this wicked witch-woman feasted on his body until there was nothing left.

When the hunter did not return the tribe thought he had been killed on the hunt. They planted the sacred poles in front of his shelter and performed the dance for the dead. However, after a while they noticed that whenever a lone blackfellow went on the hunt he did not return. Then the people became fearful and there was much talk.

'Time was when there was always something left of the ones killed in the forest. Now we find no body, no offering to return to our Mother Earth,' said a seasoned hunter.

Up spoke an old woman: 'It is true that spirit women seek husbands among our men.'

'And it is true also that bunyips lure men into swamps and rivers,' suggested another.

But no one could tell the fate of these men, not even the wise ones. Something was stopping their seeing power.

'There lies evil behind the darkness. Be wary in all places and let many travel together when they go far from camp. No one should walk alone at night,' they advised.

So the blackfellows hunted in large parties, and the warriors avoided the forest when they scouted the enemy's movements. Each man wore a bracelet with his totem carved on it to keep him from danger.

One day Burryan the great hunter was returning to camp when he spotted something moving high up in a tree. It was a large furry beast with a very long tail which it used to swing from tree to tree. Burryan wondered if this animal was the one that killed the hunters. It certainly looked powerful enough to lift a man into a tree and crush his body.

He was determined to find out where the creature rested. He followed a path which led deeper and deeper into the forest. Suddenly the path ended. Beyond was a tangle of vines, woody shrubs and great big tamarind trees with thick girths. He could go no further.

Meanwhile daylight had faded.

Too late the warrior remembered the warning of the wise one.

Too late he began to retrace his steps in the dark cold forest.

He gripped his spear tightly as he tried to find a way out.

Suddenly Burryan stops.

Something is following him.

He crouches behind a tree . . . waiting . . .

watching.

Stealthy footsteps approach.

The warrior springs, spear poised, ready to strike . . . and is astonished to see . . . a young woman.

Yes, the wireenun, the witch-woman of the forest.

'Why do you walk at night in such a place?' enquired Burryan.

'All of forest is my home. I know it well,' retorted the woman.

'Great danger waits in forest. Many men go in, they do not come out. Yet none see how they die,' said Burryan.

'Na, I do not fear. I am only a poor weak woman,' she teased.

'Beasts do not know man from woman. All is one to a hungry beast,' said Burryan angrily. 'Come, let I walk with you to your shelter.'

The woman led the way and soon they came to a dwelling with a roof of woven grass, and walls made of stout poles latched together with strong vines and plastered over with mud.

She invited Burryan to her fire place, 'My humpy is open to you. Come, sit near my fire.'

Burryan hesitated. He was uneasy.

What kind of woman would live alone in a place so full of danger?

Was she a wireenun as the wise women said?

The woman saw his face clouded with doubt. She turned her smiling face on him and said:

> 'Here is no danger
> Here walls are tight and strong
> Here not a one come in
> Less I wish.'

Burryan entered.

While the woman busied herself preparing a meal Burryan looked around her shelter. He had not seen such clever weaving before. Dried seaweed covered the mud floor and as he moved around, his foot touched something smooth. He bent and picked up a bracelet of stones. On the largest stone was a carving of a snake. It was the totem of one of the hunters who had not returned. Quickly Burryan placed it in his dillybag.

Outside the woman was mixing a potion of juices squeezed from fruits and roots over a fire. She closed her eyes as she chanted strange words in a low tuneless voice. After some time she sniffed it and smiled but her eyes were cold and bright.

'It is well,' she murmured:
　'Deep sleep come soon
　And when full moon fill black forest with
　　white light
　This one, he go to never-ending night.'
The sweet-smelling brew filled the room as the woman placed the meal before Burryan.

''Tis a hot brew. Drink fast lest it grow cold,' she commanded.

'Bring water also to cool the mouth after I drink,' said Burryan.

By the time the woman returned he was eating the delicious turtle eggs she had cooked him.

Long before they finished the meal Burryan

appeared drowsy.

'Night is far gone and my eyes fill with night dust. Let I sleep here in your safe shelter,' begged Burryan.

'Sa, sa. It is right to do so,' the woman replied eagerly. 'See a bed so soft, so warm. You will rest well.'

She led him to a mat woven from the padanus palm tree, and gloated as she watched him try to put one unsteady foot in front of the other, and slump on to the mat. He looked foolish and weak lying there, his mouth hanging open, his chest rising and falling in time with the strangled sounds coming from his throat. Gone was Burryan the great hunter.

The woman went about her business as though she had all the time in the world. She could see that the man was well-drugged. When the gunnai was as sharp as flints, she returned to the humpy and to the man-prey she had caught.

There he was lying as she left him
lying on his back with his legs
sprawled open lying with his eyes fast
closed lying in sleep
waiting for death.

She raised the gunnai high and brought it swiftly down, aimed at his heart. But the man sprang up for he had not drunk the drugged juice. He snatched the gunnai from her hand, the same gunnai she would kill him with. He turned it on her and thrust it straight into her heart. In that moment when the gunnai found her heart she was changed into a spider by Biamee, the Great Father of all who allows nothing to be destroyed.

In the forest the wireenun still weaves her web to catch unwary victims.

Why Kwaku Ananse has a Narrow Waist

In Ghana there are many stories about Kwaku Ananse the spider which are known as Anansesem or spider stories. Why the spider has a narrow waist is my version of an Ananse story told me by Amoafi Kwapong, a Ghanaian storyteller.

6
Why Kwaku Ananse has a Narrow Waist

Listen to the story.

Once upon a time in Africa – and a very good time it was – there was one Kwaku Ananse who was sometimes a man and sometimes a spider. Ananse the spider was round and fat all over. Now this Ananse had two sons. The first boy was called Ntikuma, and the second was called Efu Doshay Doshay.

One day, in the time of a great hunger, Ananse called his two sons and said, 'My children, if we do not eat soon we shall die. There is nothing here so I have thought of a plan. You must both go and find food.'

'Pappa, where shall we go?' asked the elder boy.

'I will tie this rope around my middle. You,

Ntikuma, will take one end of the rope and follow the road to the East where your cousins are holding a yam-feast. When the food is ready to be shared, you must tug on the rope so that I may come and partake of the feast.'

'It will be as you say, Pappa,' said Ntikuma.

'And you, Efu Doshay Doshay, must take the opposite path which leads to the West. You will find a village where wealthy people store their crops and food in large barns. Sniff well and when you find such a barn, tug on the rope so that I may come and share in the food.'

'I will do as you say, Pappa,' said Efu Doshay Doshay. And the two departed, one to the East and one to the West.

Long, long, Ananse waited with the rope tied around his middle. Suddenly he felt a tug from the East. Ananse chanted:

'In the East is food a-plenty
There I'll go and fill my belly.'

He set out to join Ntikuma at the feast in the East. But he hadn't gone far when he felt another tug, from the West.

'What! can it be that Efu Doshay Doshay has found food already,' he exclaimed. And he chanted:

'In the West is food a-plenty
There I'll go and fill my belly.'

But now he couldn't decide which way to go.
'East or West
Which is best?'
he asked himself.

His sons were tugging on the rope, first one, then the other and they pulled Ananse this way and that way. Then, from each end, both sons tugged hard at the same time.

'Aiye! Aiye!' Ananse screamed. He felt the rope cutting through his body.

'Help! Help!' The rope was squeezing the breath out of his body. Just then his wife Aso returned from visiting her relatives. She saw what was happening and quickly cut the rope on either side, and set Ananse free.

What a change in Ananse! The rope had pinched so tightly, that now a narrow band divided his once round body into two parts.

'What a waste!' he cried when he saw his new shape.

He was bemoaning the loss of his firm rounded flesh, but Aso thought he meant the narrow band, and ever after she called it Ananse's waist.

So you see how Ananse came to have a thin waist. It was all because of his greed.

A Woven Testament

*In the Greek myth Athene's revenge
on Arachne always puzzled me
leaving me vaguely dissatisfied. I
could not understand why a girl as
talented as Arachne should lose faith
in her skill. Or why a goddess should
feel so threatened by a mere mortal.
When I discovered that Athene had
caused monstrous transformations in
at least two other persons I saw both
Athene and Arachne in a new
light . . .*

7
A Woven Testament

i

Yesterday I hanged myself.

she offered me life on her terms but I said I would choose death rather than give up weaving which is all of life to me.

'No, not death,' *she* said, smiling her cold beautiful smile, 'for that would make you immortal and one of the very gods you claim to despise.'

Then *she* looked at me with veiled eyes so that I could not read her thoughts but I felt the hate *she* bore me, hate so intense that I trembled and turned away from her.

The people worship her, their goddess, their benefactress, their Athene. They are simple folk who confuse patronage with love, and beauty with virtue. There are a few who know the truth but their silence is a conspiracy which allows these Olympians to call themselves gods. My father believed them to be no more than heroes, mortals who excel at skills, or are endowed with outstanding physical attributes, and I hold to his belief. He often said, 'They are heroes who achieve excellence and to this end all should strive. But a god must be able to create and that requires wisdom.'

My father brought this creed with him from the land of his ancestors in the East. He said his people were encouraged to seek wisdom above all things. And he inspired my quest for wisdom through excellence. It was he who gave me my first lessons in spinning and weaving. In his country he was a noble lord with many ships at his command. He came to Greece to trade silks and fell in love with my mother. Since she would not leave her land he stayed here.

'*she* has a gift from the gods,' *she* said to my father. *she* was looking at one of my tapestries which had been chosen for a festival in our town.

'No, it is not a gift but mine. I did it myself,' I said with all the artlessness of a seven-year-old. 'I am striving for excellence.'

she laughed and patted my cheek and her hands were hot and dry.

'What is your name, child?' *she* enquired.

'I am called Lydia,' I replied.

'Well, Lydia,' *she* said, 'excellence belongs only to the gods. It is we who have granted you this gift of weaving and we can take it away from you.'

That was our first meeting.

My father died when I was eleven.

Before he died he said to me, 'You have learned well how to imitate. Now you must learn how to create. But first practise the art of looking.'

He taught me how to become still and to look with all of myself until I saw through out-side to in-side of things. Looking through-out gave me new insight and a new understanding. It was as though I was centred on whatever I gazed upon. I discovered new worlds. In those hidden worlds colours glowed with a brilliance I had not seen before. Whatever I wove took on a life of its own. Images expressed themselves in movement and form I could neither control nor define.

All over the country artisans and adjudicators debated my new style of picture-weaving. The aristoi, wealthy landowners, did not wait on their verdict but ordered elaborately designed hangings and canopies for their town houses. The merchants, following their lead, traded my tapestries in lands near and far. I became famous.

'Surely this is not the offering of any mortal!' *she* stated.

she was attending the opening ceremony of a new temple dedicated to her and the temple officials were showing her a full-length wall hanging I had given. The motif was a body, part human, part serpentine, in the act of uncoiling. It was a study of exquisite form but it was the eyes which dominated the picture. One eye was dark and heavy-lidded and from the other pale blue eye there came a beam of golden light. The two combined to produce a startling effect on the beholder.

No one dared answer for fear of seeming to contradict her.

'Whose work is this?' *she* asked imperiously.

'It is mine,' I said.

she looked closely at my face.

'We have met before,' she said with certainty. *she* never forgot a face, so the people said. In any case *she* could hardly forget mine. My almond-shaped eyes, long straight black hair, and fine bones, marked my Eastern heritage.

'You once described my skill at weaving as a gift from the gods.'

'Ah yes! You are the one who strives for excellence,' *she* recalled. 'And now that you have achieved it what will you strive for next?'

'I want to create,' I said.

'So! You desire to become a god! Perhaps even to dwell on Mount Olympos!' *she* was goading me, trying to make me look foolish in the eyes of the people. I was too young to understand why. Had I understood I might have bridled my tongue.

'What I desire is more than the excellence of Olympians. It is the wisdom to create,' I retorted.

The silence which filled the hall was like a mist obscuring everyone else leaving only *she* and I, two adversaries, facing each other. A mask of superiority slid into place but not before I glimpsed puckers of bewilderment around her eyes and knew that *she* did not fully understand what I meant.

When *she* spoke her words were barbed and swift as arrows sped from a bow. 'The wisdom of the ages! You, a mortal, would usurp that which not even all the gods possess! Do you not know, child, that those mortals are cursed who are allowed to know it? It is a duty placed on crones, women who are loathsome to men and scorned by their own kind. The gods pity such unfortunates and grant them solace through wisdom. Beware lest ambition destroy you.'

That was our second meeting.

It was just two days later that I saw *her* walking through our olive grove.

'I am here as messenger,' *she* announced.

I waited and tried as best I could, to hide the shock at seeing *her* in a private place.

'Your weaving has pleased the gods and it is their wish that you receive the official accolade you have earned. They insist that your work be given its rightful place in the sphere of the Arts.'

'I am honoured to know that my work is worthy of such recognition,' I said. I chose my words with care. After our encounter at the temple my mother had warned me. 'Beware!' she said. 'Athene is an unyielding warrior and *she* claims the attributes of wisdom. You present a threat to her.'

she was watching me intently, the way a cat watches a mouse when the victim has no escape. *she* continued, 'The gods have set out terms which will allow your work to be seen by all for its true worth when it is placed next to my own.' *she* had issued her challenge.

If I refused I would be branded a coward and ridiculed. If I agreed I would be considered an arrogant upstart for pitting myself against the gods. I saw the barely concealed sneer on her face and said:

'I accept.'

Only then did *she* tell me that the chosen theme was to be the gods and that the weaving was to be completed in the next six days!

Six days later the judges met. They crowded around her frieze.

Her work was to be judged first for she was the supreme craftswoman, and my work would be judged against hers. Neither of us had seen the other's weaving but I could guess from what I overheard that *her* pictures told the story of *her* contest with Poseidon. When I was finally allowed to look I had to admit that *her* position as patroness of the Arts was well-deserved. The horse, which Poseidon is said to have created, appeared as a creature perfectly formed and of noble stature. It was night-black, and the powerful muscles seemed to ripple in readiness for flight as it emerged from the ground where Poseidon struck his staff.

In contrast *she* had also woven scenes of a couple from youth to death showing how at each stage the olive tree and its fruit were used for the good of human beings, and *she* had enclosed the scenes with beautiful borders of olive branches covered with white flowers and shiny black fruit.

I had been so absorbed in *her* weaving that I

had not noticed how the Olympians were responding to my own until I heard a roar of laughter which could only have come from Zeus. I looked across at the group of judges and saw that the others were unwilling to share his judgement. They had every right to hesitate for I had enshrined in the sections of an intricate pattern I had invented called a web, incidents in the life of Zeus.

'Here is one who truly understands the cravings of the heart,' Zeus said. 'In every act, in every feature and form there is animation, life, feeling. We see ourselves as never before. Not just excellent pictures but creations.'

Zeus their leader had pronounced and everyone looked and listened with awe. My head was ringing and those words of praise were to bring comfort in the darkest night of my existence. As soon as I could, I fled from the great hall. I wanted to be alone, to savour the moment of my first step towards creating. I did not even care about the final judging.

I had made a vow that I would not pay homage to the Olympians through my craft. But what could I weave? There seemed to be no theme I could present which would not entrap me. I wanted to give up the whole affair and suffer the consequences. Then I heard my father's voice as clearly as though he were alive. He was talking about the Olympians.

'As children snatch at flowers one minute and thrust them aside the next, so do they with their pleasure.'

An idea was born. I would illustrate the pleasures of Zeus.

In each section of the web there is a picture of Zeus in one of his many guises. Zeus in the form of a hawk stealing Io who is tethered to an olive tree; Zeus as a bull abducting Europa whose expression is one of smug satisfaction rather than fear; Zeus stealing away from Hera, who is fast asleep, to the nymph Maia in her cave; Zeus in the form of a swan pursuing Leda, and Zeus in his divine form snatching an embryo from the womb of the smouldering Semele. Whatever his disguise Zeus wears an expression of a child who takes his pleasures lightly and whose eyes are bright with desire. In each vignette one eye is already turned to the next object of his fancy.

'Were you so sure of success that you did not await the verdict?' *she* accused me.

I turned and saw her. *she* had followed me to my private sanctum, my father's catacomb.

'Zeus has been generous in his praise for your work. He chooses to see only humour and vigour. However, others see your attempt to humiliate the gods and for this blasphemy you shall publicly announce your decision to cease from weaving. But first you will take a vow on your father's tomb never to touch a loom or spin a thread.'

How long I stood there speechless, I do not know but when I regained my senses I found that my head was moving from side to side as though controlled by an unseen hand.

'I will appeal to Zeus himself,' I cried.

'Fidelity is not one of Zeus's virtues as you so skilfully pointed out in your weaving. He has already forgotten you and placed your future in my hands,' *she* retaliated.

'I will not yield to your demands,' I said. 'I would rather die than give up my weaving.'

Although I was filled with anger I had no fear of her until *she* locked me in the tomb.

'I will fetch your weaving so that you may destroy it with your own hands,' *she* said.

106

Such total disgrace would be for me the same as a dishonourable death. I would rob her of the satisfaction of seeing me suffer. I had brought my bag of silk threads with me. I plaited many strands together so that they were doubly strong. Then I stood on a plinth and looped a length of silk over one of the beams in the tomb. The rest I wound around my legs, my waist, and under my arm. Then I twisted the remainder tightly around my neck and sprung off the plinth.

At that moment *she* re-entered the tomb and saw me swinging in the air bound with silken thread. The thread was cutting into my neck and my waist but I was still alive. Her eyes widened with the shock of seeing me in such a state. *she* reached up to free me, pau ed, and changed her mind.

'You shall not die but live for your weaving,' *she* said. 'And since you wish for the wisdom to become a creator, that too will be granted. But I warned you of the price you must pay for wisdom.'

she sprinkled liquid from a phial over me. It had a bitter taste and a sickly smell. In that instant my limbs felt lifeless, my body began to shrink and my senses were in a state of chaos. I opened my mouth to cry, 'Help me!' but no words came. I heard her voice as though from a

long way off and the words were intoned:
    'Spin! Spin! Spin!
    Arachne you be.
    You shall create works of great beauty
    Yet be an object of pity.

    Spin! Spin! Spin!
    Arachne you be.
    Men shall repel you
    Women seek to destroy you
    And you shall devour your kin.
    Spin! Spin! Spin!'

I have spent a night of horror and my fears are so great that death would be deliverance. I do not know what I have become. Colours fade and I can no longer discern shapes. I feel my way about. The body moves to find food. The mind revolts against what it finds yet I am urged to eat.

I know that whatever spell *she* cast over me has come to pass. That I am hideous to behold and repulsive to others. And that is why I shall hide in places where none can see me. *she* has robbed me of everything that is human except my skill and I use that now to tell my story. I pray that someone finds this woven testament of my fate so that all may know that *she* is no goddess.

she is no heroine
Athene is a bitch

She is a Witch

Grace Hallworth

MOUTH OPEN, STORY JUMP OUT

Late at night, when the moon is full, you may find your path barred by a man whose body stretches into the sky. Know, then, that you have met the Moongazer and turn back before it's too late.

And if your journey takes you through the forest, avoid the gaze of the lost children whose faces have no features.

Grace Hallworth spins a spellbinding web of tales in this enthralling collection of stories from the people of Trinidad and Tobago.